How Do I Love Thee?

Jennifer Adams · Christopher Silas Neal

BALZER + BRAY
An Imprint of HarperCollins*Publishers*

Balzer + Bray is an imprint of HarperCollins Publishers.

How Do I Love Thee?
Text copyright © 2018 by Jennifer Adams
Illustrations copyright © 2018 by Christopher Silas Neal
All rights reserved. Manufactured in China.

ISBN 978-0-06-239444-6

The artist used mixed media and digital to create the illustrations for this book.
Typography by Dana Fritts and Christopher Silas Neal
18 19 20 21 22 SCP 10 9 8 7 6 5 4 3 2 1
❖

First Edition

For Bill. I love you in all the ways.

—J. A.

For Jasper, River, and Jen.

—C. S. N.

How do I love thee?

Let me count the ways.

I love thee deep

and wide and high.

I love thee in soft sunlight

and rain-drizzled night.

I love thee
with a whisper

and a song

and a *ROAR*.

And when out of sight

and in every day's most quiet needs.

I love thee by stars

and firelight.

By spring's first snowdrops

and fall's red trees

and winter's frost-etched breath.

I love thee with all my smiles

and tears.

I love thee when first you wake

and at end of day's
goodnight kiss.

And I will always love thee.

Elizabeth Barrett Browning was born on March 6, 1806. She was a famous poet in the Victorian era. Elizabeth wrote this poem to the great love of her life—her husband, Robert Browning. Robert was also a famous Victorian poet.

How do I love thee? Let me count the ways.

I love thee to the depth and breadth and height

My soul can reach, when feeling out of sight

For the ends of Being and ideal Grace.

I love thee to the level of every day's

Most quiet need, by sun and candle-light.

I love thee freely, as men strive for Right;

I love thee purely, as they turn from Praise.

I love thee with a passion put to use

In my old griefs, and with my childhood's faith.

I love thee with a love I seemed to lose

With my lost saints, — I love thee with the breath,

Smiles, tears, of all my life! — and, if God choose,

I shall but love thee better after death.